My MANGA Journal

Name _____

Address _____

_____

Contact _____

_____

DAVID & CHARLES

www.davidandcharles.com

Key

Fill in the boxes with your own symbols for events and tasks, then use this as a key for your journal!

	To-Do
	Box-Sets
	Exam
	Birthday
	Party
	Important
	Done
	Postponed
	Cancelled

Index

Future log

JANUARY

M	T	W	T	F	S	S

FEBRUARY

M	T	W	T	F	S	S

MARCH

M	T	W	T	F	S	S

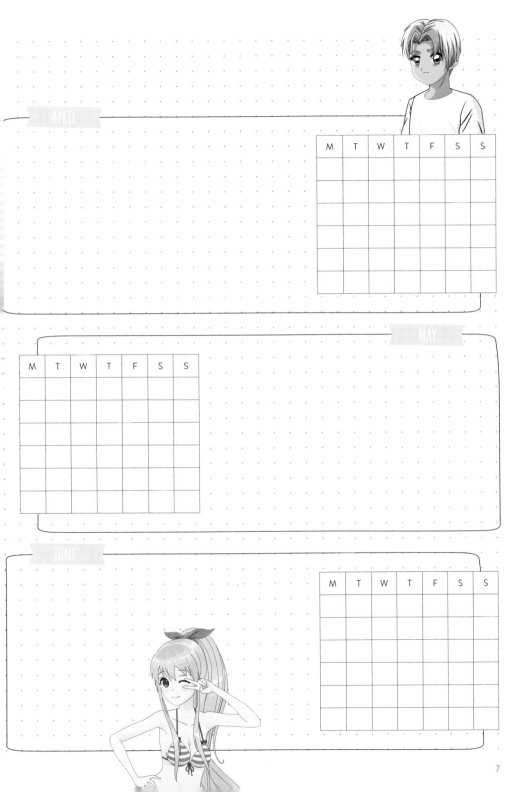

APRIL

M	T	W	T	F	S	S

MAY

M	T	W	T	F	S	S

JUNE

M	T	W	T	F	S	S

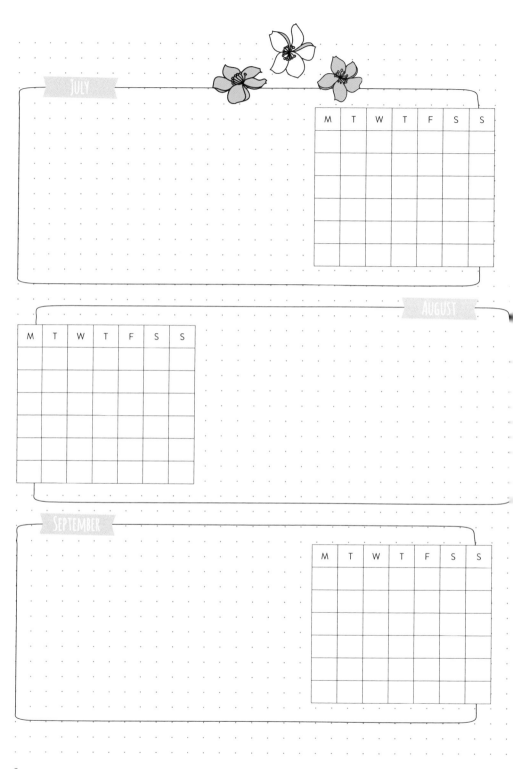

July

M	T	W	T	F	S	S

August

M	T	W	T	F	S	S

September

M	T	W	T	F	S	S

October

M	T	W	T	F	S	S

November

M	T	W	T	F	S	S

December

M	T	W	T	F	S	S

Weekly Schedule

Time	Monday	Tuesday	Wednesday	Thursday	Friday

TIME	MONDAY	TUESDAY	WEDNESDAY	THURSDAY	FRIDAY

Habit Tracker

My Sports Goal..................... (e.g. 3 times per week)
My Learning Goal:................   My ....Goal: ....

Week	Sport	Learning	....
1.			
2.			
3.			
4.			
5.			
6.			
7.			
8.			
9.			
10.			
11.			
12.			
13.			
14.			
15.			
16.			
17.			
18.			
19.			
20.			
21.			
22.			

23.		
24.		
25.		
26.		
27.		
28.		
29.		
30.		
31.		
32.		
33.		
34.		
35.		
36.		
37.		
38.		
39.		
40.		
41.		
42.		
43.		
44.		
45.		
46.		
47.		
48.		
49.		
50.		
51.		
52.		
53.		

My Teachers

Keep all the details of your teachers or professors in this handy section.

SUBJECT:..
TEACHER:..
EMAIL:..
ROOM:..

SUBJECT:..

TEACHER:...

EMAIL:...

ROOM:..

SUBJECT:..

TEACHER:...

EMAIL:...

ROOM:..

SUBJECT:..

TEACHER:...

EMAIL:...

ROOM:..

SUBJECT:..

TEACHER:...

EMAIL:...

ROOM:..

Monthly Overview

1
2
3
4
5
6
7
8
9
10
11
12
13
14
15
16
17
18
19
20
21
22
23
24
25
26
27
28
29
30
31

WEEK

Monday	Tuesday	Wednesday

TO-DO

TO-DO

TO-DO

NOTES

Thursday

Friday

Saturday

TO-DO

TO-DO

Sunday

Monday	Tuesday	Wednesday

To-Do	To-Do	To-Do

Beauty is in the eye of the beholder

Thursday

Friday

Saturday

TO-DO

TO-DO

Sunday

NOTES

WEEK

Monday

Tuesday

Wednesday

To-Do

To-Do

To-Do

NOTES

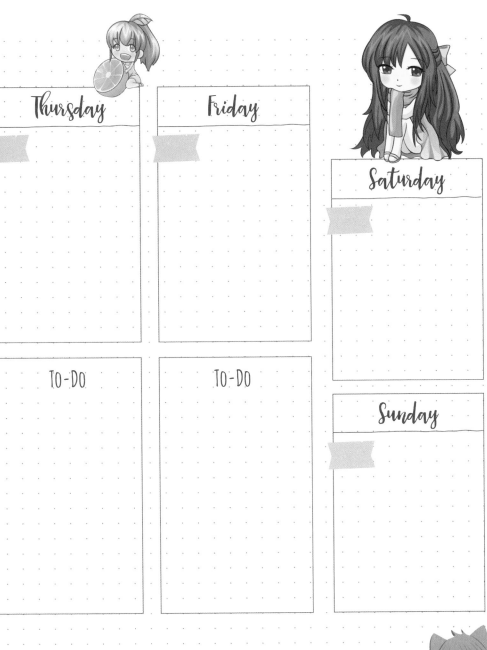

Thursday

Friday

Saturday

TO-DO

TO-DO

Sunday

All plans start without a plan

Monday

Tuesday

Wednesday

TO-DO

TO-DO

TO-DO

When nothing is sure,
everything is possible

MARGARETH DABBLE

Thursday

Friday

Saturday

To-Do

To-Do

Sunday

NOTES

Books List

Write down all the books (or Manga comics) you
want to read and then give them a star rating
once you have.

○ _____

○ _____

○ _____

○ _____

○ _____

○ _____

○ _____

○ _____

○ _____

○ _____

○ _____

○ _____

○ _____

○ _____

○ _____

○ _____

○ _____

○ _____

○ _____

Monthly Overview

1
2
3
4
5
6
7
8
9
10
11
12
13
14
15
16
17
18
19
20
21
22
23
24
25
26
27
28
29
30
31

WEEK

Monday

Tuesday

Wednesday

TO-DO

TO-DO

TO-DO

NOTES

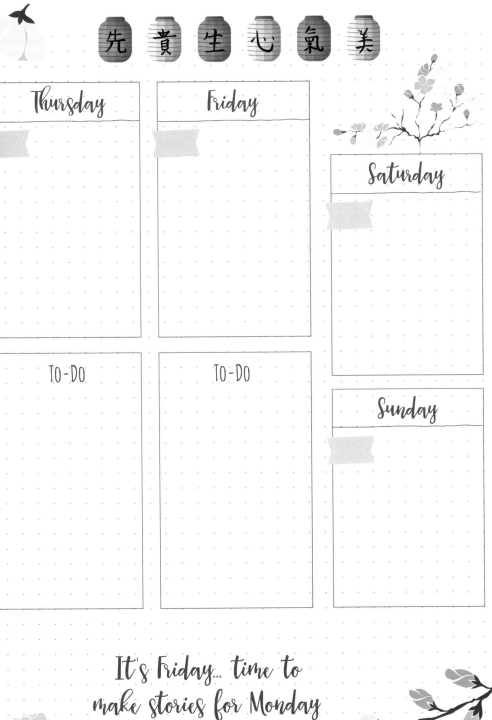

先 貴 生 心 氣 美

Thursday

Friday

Saturday

TO-DO

TO-DO

Sunday

It's Friday... time to make stories for Monday

Monday

Tuesday

Wednesday

TO-DO

TO-DO

TO-DO

NOTES

Thursday

Friday

Saturday

TO-DO

TO-DO

Sunday

WEEK

Monday

Tuesday

Wednesday

TO-DO

TO-DO

TO-DO

Thursday

Friday

Saturday

To-Do

To-Do

Sunday

Notes

Monday

Tuesday

Wednesday

To-Do

To-Do

To-Do

Notes

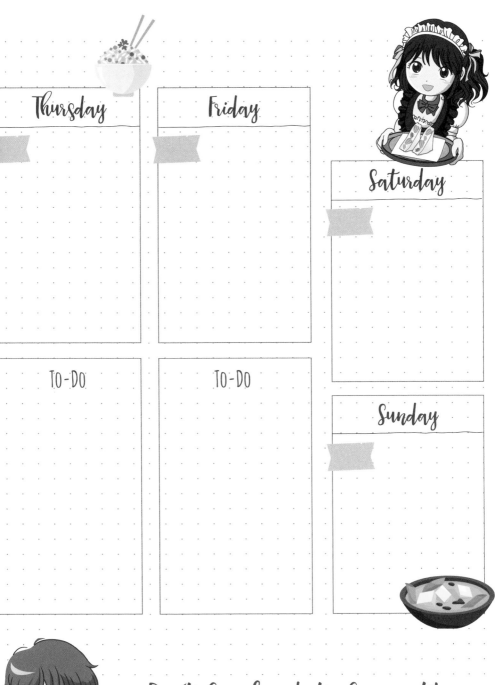

Thursday

Friday

Saturday

TO-DO

TO-DO

Sunday

Don't be afraid to be great!

Notes

What's on your mind? Doodle it here!

1
2
3
4
5
6
7
8
9
10
11
12
13
14
15
16
17
18
19
20
21
22
23
24
25
26
27
28
29
30
31

Monday	Tuesday	Wednesday

TO-DO	TO-DO	TO-DO

We all have to think,
so why not think positive?

Thursday

Friday

Saturday

Sunday

To-Do

To-Do

Notes

Week

Monday

Tuesday

Wednesday

To-Do

To-Do

To-Do

Notes

Thursday

Friday

Saturday

TO-DO

TO-DO

Sunday

Sometimes we're so quick to count the days that we forget to make the days count

Week

Monday

Tuesday

Wednesday

To-Do

To-Do

To-Do

If travelling were free,
you'd never see me again

Thursday

Friday

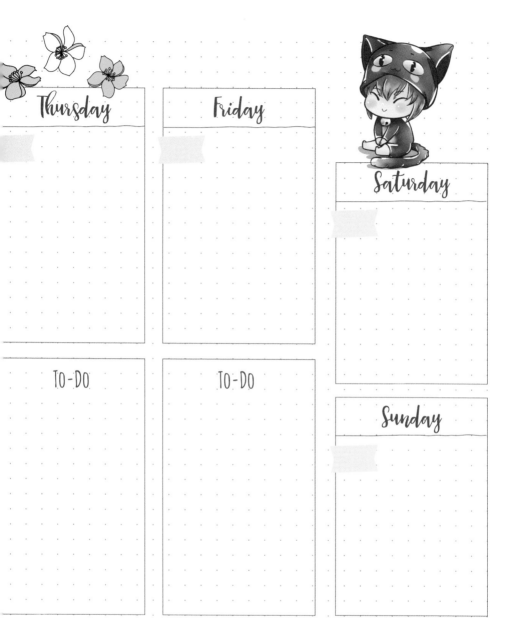

Saturday

To-Do

To-Do

Sunday

Notes

WEEK

Monday

Tuesday

Wednesday

TO-DO

TO-DO

TO-DO

NOTES

Thursday

Friday

Saturday

TO-DO

TO-DO

Sunday

Be like a pineapple - stand
up straight, wear a crown
and be sweet on the inside!

My Bucket List: BFF-Edition

Experience new adventures! You've probably already planned lots of great things to do with your friends. Write them down here so you don't forget them!

- ○ _____
- ○ _____
- ○ _____
- ○ _____
- ○ _____
- ○ _____
- ○ _____
- ○ _____
- ○ _____
- ○ _____
- ○ _____
- ○ _____
- ○ _____
- ○ _____
- ○ _____
- ○ _____
- ○ _____

Must-Haves

When you have no money, you can think of loads of things you'd like, but then when the time comes you can't remember any of them! If this sounds familiar, why not write down all your shopping wants here?

MUST-HAVE	PURPOSE	PRICE	BOUGHT!

1
2
3
4
5
6
7
8
9
10
11
12
13
14
15
16
17
18
19
20
21
22
23
24
25
26
27
28
29
30
31

WEEK

Monday

Tuesday

Wednesday

TO-DO

TO-DO

TO-DO

NOTES

Thursday

Friday

Saturday

To-Do

To-Do

Sunday

Creativity is intelligence having fun

ALBERT EINSTEIN

Monday

Tuesday

Wednesday

To-Do

To-Do

To-Do

Thursday

Friday

Saturday

Sunday

To-Do

To-Do

NOTES

Monday

Tuesday

Wednesday

TO-DO

TO-DO

TO-DO

NOTES

Thursday

Friday

Saturday

TO-DO

TO-DO

Sunday

Some days you just have to
create your own sunshine

WEEK

Monday	Tuesday	Wednesday

TO-DO	TO-DO	TO-DO

NOTES

Thursday

Friday

Saturday

TO-DO

TO-DO

Sunday

My Bucket List

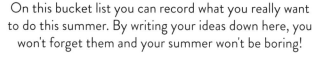

On this bucket list you can record what you really want
to do this summer. By writing your ideas down here, you
won't forget them and your summer won't be boring!

○ _____

○ _____

○ _____

○ _____

○ _____

○ _____

○ _____

○ _____

○ _____

○ _____

○ _____

○ _____

○ _____

○ _____

○ _____

○ _____

○ _____

My Bucket List: Dreams-Edition

Are there things you really want to do in the next few years? What dreams do you want to fulfil? Write them down here and then tick them off!

- ○ _____
- ○ _____
- ○ _____
- ○ _____
- ○ _____
- ○ _____
- ○ _____
- ○ _____
- ○ _____
- ○ _____
- ○ _____
- ○ _____
- ○ _____
- ○ _____
- ○ _____
- ○ _____
- ○ _____

1
2
3
4
5
6
7
8
9
10
11
12
13
14
15
16
17
18
19
20
21
22
23
24
25
26
27
28
29
30
31

WEEK

Monday

Tuesday

Wednesday

TO-DO

TO-DO

TO-DO

Thinking is difficult, that's
why most people judge

CARL JUNG

Thursday

Friday

Saturday

To-Do

To-Do

Sunday

Notes

Monday

Tuesday

Wednesday

To-Do

To-Do

To-Do

NOTES

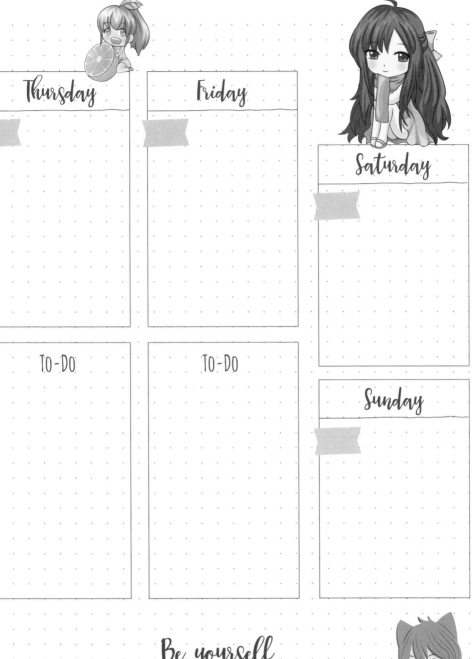

Thursday

Friday

Saturday

TO-DO

TO-DO

Sunday

Be yourself.
Everyone else already exists

Monday

Tuesday

Wednesday

To-Do

To-Do

To-Do

Thursday

Friday

Saturday

TO-DO

TO-DO

Sunday

NOTES

Monday

Tuesday

Wednesday

TO-DO

TO-DO

TO-DO

NOTES

Thursday

Friday

Saturday

To-Do

To-Do

Sunday

Follow your dreams, they know the way

Cool DIY Projects

Make a list of things you want to make: it could be
recipes, craft projects or upcycling ideas... go!

Loaned and Borrowed

Keep track of all the things you have either loaned to friends or borrowed yourself.

Object	Borrowed	Loaned	To/From	Returned

Always lend a helping hand

1
2
3
4
5
6
7
8
9
10
11
12
13
14
15
16
17
18
19
20
21
22
23
24
25
26
27
28
29
30
31

WEEK

Monday

Tuesday

Wednesday

TO-DO

TO-DO

TO-DO

NOTES

Thursday

Friday

Saturday

TO-DO

TO-DO

Sunday

Don't Worry, be Happy!

WEEK

Monday

Tuesday

Wednesday

To-Do

To-Do

To-Do

Go outside and
get some sunshine

Thursday

Friday

Saturday

TO-DO

TO-DO

Sunday

NOTES

Monday

Tuesday

Wednesday

To-Do

To-Do

To-Do

Notes

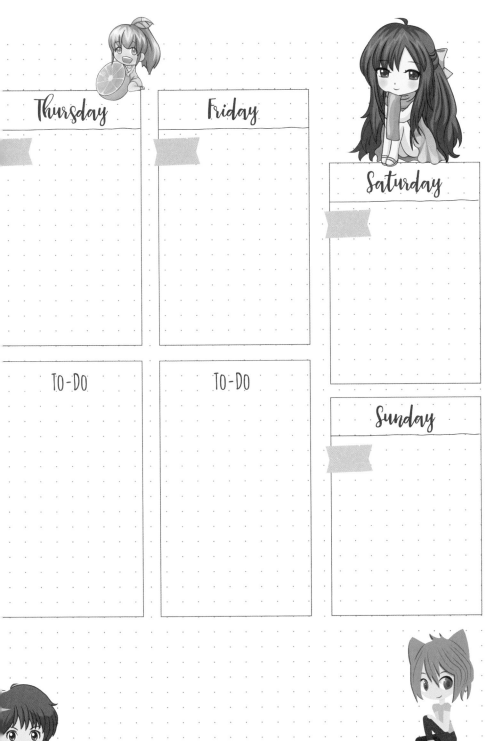

Thursday

Friday

Saturday

TO-DO

TO-DO

Sunday

WEEK

Monday

Tuesday

Wednesday

To-Do

To-Do

To-Do

You are somebody special

Thursday

Friday

Saturday

TO-DO

TO-DO

Sunday

NOTES

My Box-Sets and Animes

Which box-sets and and animes do
you really want to watch?

○ _____
○ _____
○ _____
○ _____
○ _____
○ _____
○ _____
○ _____
○ _____
○ _____
○ _____
○ _____
○ _____
○ _____
○ _____
○ _____
○ _____

My Travels

Where do you want to visit?

○ _____
○ _____
○ _____
○ _____
○ _____
○ _____
○ _____
○ _____
○ _____
○ _____
○ _____
○ _____
○ _____
○ _____
○ _____
○ _____
○ _____

Monthly Overview

1
2
3
4
5
6
7
8
9
10
11
12
13
14
15
16
17
18
19
20
21
22
23
24
25
26
27
28
29
30
31

Monday

Tuesday

Wednesday

TO-DO

TO-DO

TO-DO

NOTES

Thursday

Friday

Saturday

TO-DO

TO-DO

Sunday

Let's explore this awesome world

WEEK

Monday

Tuesday

Wednesday

TO-DO

TO-DO

TO-DO

NOTES

Thursday

Friday

Saturday

TO-DO

TO-DO

Sunday

Coffee in one hand,
confidence in the other

Monday

Tuesday

Wednesday

To-Do

To-Do

To-Do

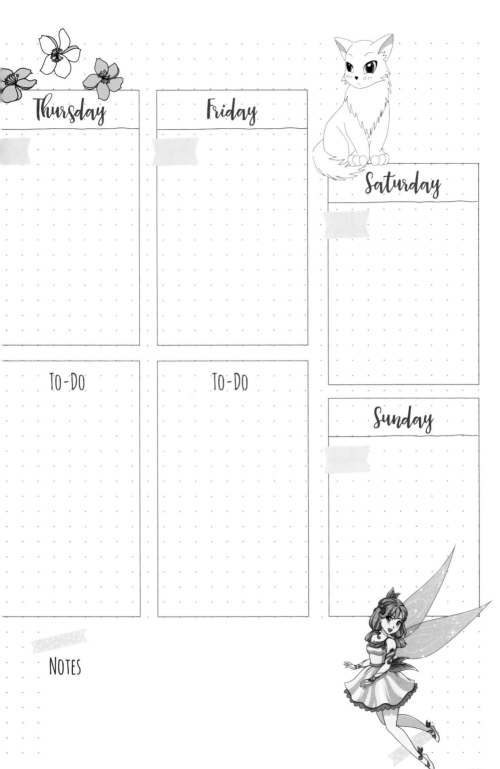

Thursday

Friday

Saturday

To-Do

To-Do

Sunday

Notes

Monday

Tuesday

Wednesday

TO-DO

TO-DO

TO-DO

NOTES

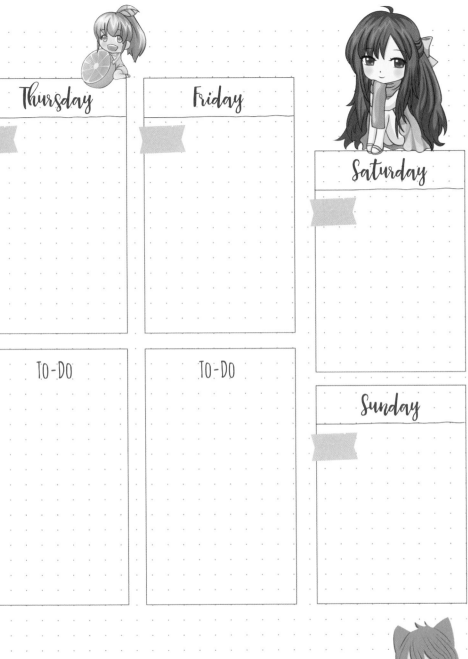

Thursday

Friday

Saturday

TO-DO

TO-DO

Sunday

Every day is a fresh start

Let's Play!

Banish boredom here! Why not play tic-tac-toe, hangman or battleships?

Monthly Overview

1
2
3
4
5
6
7
8
9
10
11
12
13
14
15
16
17
18
19
20
21
22
23
24
25
26
27
28
29
30
31

Monday

Tuesday

Wednesday

To-Do

To-Do

To-Do

Thursday

Friday

Saturday

To-Do

To-Do

Sunday

NOTES

Monday

Tuesday

Wednesday

TO-DO

TO-DO

TO-DO

NOTES

Thursday

Friday

Saturday

TO-DO

TO-DO

Sunday

Life is art - live yours in colour

Monday

Tuesday

Wednesday

TO-DO

TO-DO

TO-DO

NOTES

Thursday

Friday

Saturday

To-Do

To-Do

Sunday

Monday	Tuesday	Wednesday

To-Do	To-Do	To-Do

She had the soul of a gypsy,
the heart of a hippie and
the spirit of a fairy

Thursday

Friday

Saturday

To-Do

To-Do

Sunday

Notes

Social Media

Plan your next posts or write down ideas!

Inspiration

Write down quotes and sayings
that you particularly like!

○ _____
○ _____
○ _____
○ _____
○ _____
○ _____
○ _____
○ _____
○ _____
○ _____
○ _____
○ _____
○ _____
○ _____
○ _____

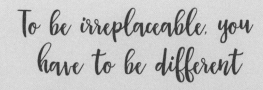

To be irreplaceable, you
have to be different

Coco Chanel

1
2
3
4
5
6
7
8
9
10
11
12
13
14
15
16
17
18
19
20
21
22
23
24
25
26
27
28
29
30
31

Week

Monday

Tuesday

Wednesday

To-Do

To-Do

To-Do

Notes

Thursday

Friday

Saturday

TO-DO

TO-DO

Sunday

| Monday | Tuesday | Wednesday |

| To-Do | To-Do | To-Do |

It is what it is but it will be what you make of it!

Thursday

Friday

Saturday

TO-DO

TO-DO

Sunday

NOTES

WEEK

Monday

Tuesday

Wednesday

To-Do

To-Do

To-Do

NOTES

Thursday

Friday

Saturday

TO-DO

TO-DO

Sunday

Enjoy the little things

Monday

Tuesday

Wednesday

To-Do

To-Do

To-Do

Notes

Thursday

Friday

Saturday

TO-DO

TO-DO

Sunday

Don't be afraid to
make mistakes

My Movies

Make a list of the films you want to watch
and then give them a star rating once you have.

○ _____ ☆ ☆ ☆ ☆ ☆

○ _____ ☆ ☆ ☆ ☆ ☆

○ _____ ☆ ☆ ☆ ☆ ☆

○ _____ ☆ ☆ ☆ ☆ ☆

○ _____ ☆ ☆ ☆ ☆ ☆

○ _____ ☆ ☆ ☆ ☆ ☆

○ _____ ☆ ☆ ☆ ☆ ☆

○ _____ ☆ ☆ ☆ ☆ ☆

○ _____ ☆ ☆ ☆ ☆ ☆

○ _____ ☆ ☆ ☆ ☆ ☆

○ _____ ☆ ☆ ☆ ☆ ☆

○ _____ ☆ ☆ ☆ ☆ ☆

○ _____ ☆ ☆ ☆ ☆ ☆

○ _____ ☆ ☆ ☆ ☆ ☆

○ _____ ☆ ☆ ☆ ☆ ☆

○ _____ ☆ ☆ ☆ ☆ ☆

○ _____ ☆ ☆ ☆ ☆ ☆

Notes

Monthly Overview

1
2
3
4
5
6
7
8
9
10
11
12
13
14
15
16
17
18
19
20
21
22
23
24
25
26
27
28
29
30
31

WEEK

Monday

Tuesday

Wednesday

To-Do

To-Do

To-Do

Storms give trees deeper roots

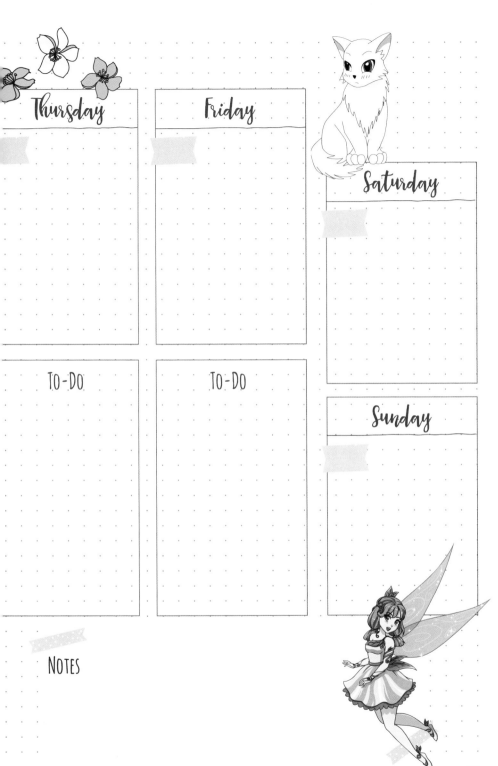

Thursday

Friday

Saturday

To-Do

To-Do

Sunday

Notes

WEEK

Monday

Tuesday

Wednesday

TO-DO

TO-DO

TO-DO

NOTES

Thursday

Friday

Saturday

TO-DO

TO-DO

Sunday

129

Monday

Tuesday

Wednesday

TO-DO

TO-DO

TO-DO

Thursday

Friday

Saturday

TO-DO

TO-DO

Sunday

NOTES

Monday

Tuesday

Wednesday

To-Do

To-Do

To-Do

Notes

Thursday

Friday

Saturday

To-Do

To-Do

Sunday

I need Google in my brain

Money Tracker

Keep track of all your expenses and income. If you want to get an exact picture for each month, simply copy this table for each month onto a new sheet of paper.

Budget

Income	Expenses	Purpose

Monthly Overview

1
2
3
4
5
6
7
8
9
10
11
12
13
14
15
16
17
18
19
20
21
22
23
24
25
26
27
28
29
30
31

WEEK

Monday

TO-DO

Tuesday

TO-DO

Wednesday

TO-DO

NOTES

Thursday

Friday

Saturday

TO-DO

TO-DO

Sunday

WEEK

Monday

Tuesday

Wednesday

TO-DO

TO-DO

TO-DO

Laughter is the best medicine

Thursday

Friday

Saturday

To-Do

To-Do

Sunday

Notes

WEEK

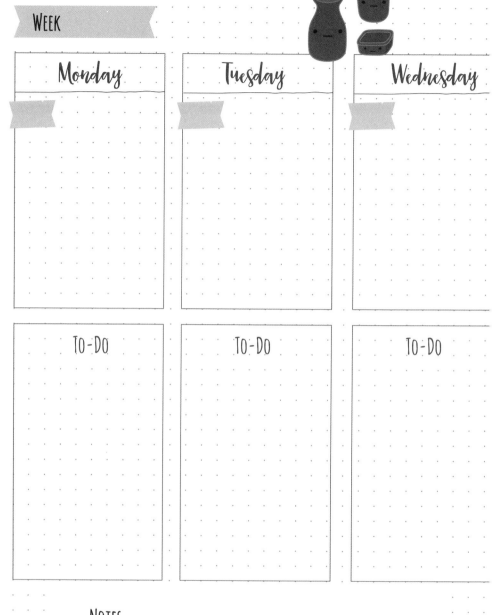

Monday

Tuesday

Wednesday

TO-DO

TO-DO

TO-DO

NOTES

Thursday

Friday

Saturday

TO-DO

TO-DO

Sunday

You can't take the lift to success
- you have to take the stairs

Monday

Tuesday

Wednesday

To-Do

To-Do

To-Do

Just because the solution is easy doesn't mean it is wrong

Thursday

Friday

Saturday

To-Do

To-Do

Sunday

NOTES

145

Monthly Overview

1
2
3
4
5
6
7
8
9
10
11
12
13
14
15
16
17
18
19
20
21
22
23
24
25
26
27
28
29
30
31

Week

Monday

Tuesday

Wednesday

To-Do

To-Do

To-Do

Notes

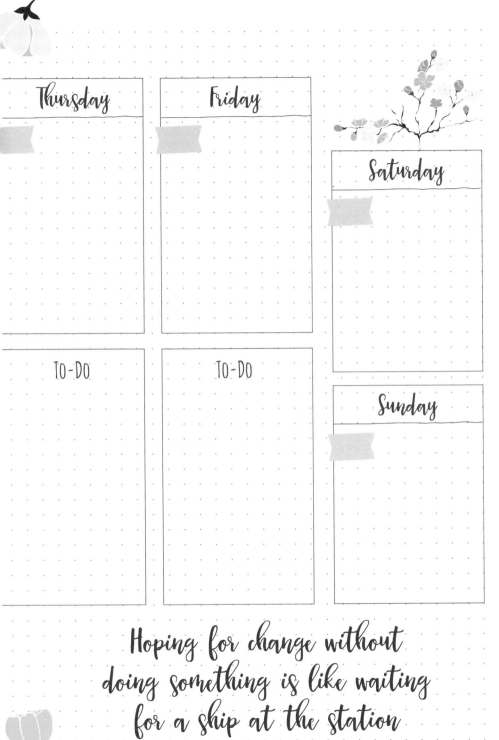

Thursday

Friday

Saturday

TO-DO

TO-DO

Sunday

Hoping for change without
doing something is like waiting
for a ship at the station

WEEK

Monday

Tuesday

Wednesday

TO-DO

TO-DO

TO-DO

NOTES

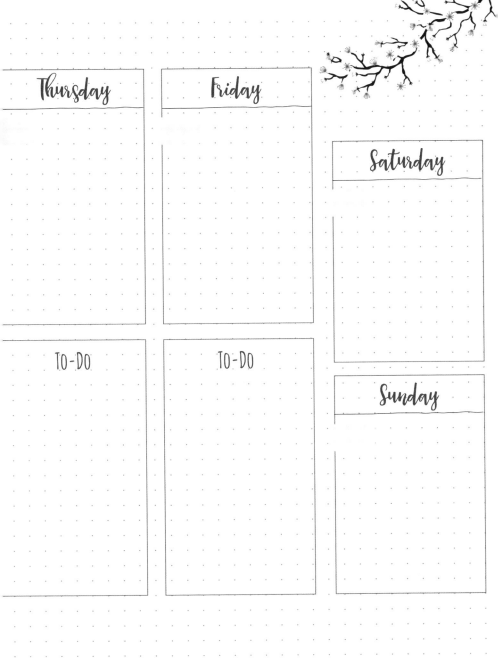

Thursday

Friday

Saturday

TO-DO

TO-DO

Sunday

WEEK

Monday

Tuesday

Wednesday

To-Do

To-Do

To-Do

When someone says
'that's impossible', remember:
these are their limits, not yours

Thursday

Friday

Saturday

TO-DO

TO-DO

Sunday

NOTES

Monday

Tuesday

Wednesday

TO-DO

TO-DO

TO-DO

NOTES

Thursday

Friday

Saturday

TO-DO

TO-DO

Sunday

Live life to the fullest every day

My Manga Art

Use this space to practise your own manga-style drawings.
Use the images throughout this journal to inspire you.

1
2
3
4
5
6
7
8
9
10
11
12
13
14
15
16
17
18
19
20
21
22
23
24
25
26
27
28
29
30
31

Monday

Tuesday

Wednesday

TO-DO

TO-DO

TO-DO

A goal without a plan is just a wish

Thursday

Friday

Saturday

TO-DO

TO-DO

Sunday

NOTES

WEEK

Monday

Tuesday

Wednesday

TO-DO

TO-DO

TO-DO

NOTES

Thursday

Friday

Saturday

Sunday

TO-DO

TO-DO

If you don't have
wings, create them

WEEK

Monday

Tuesday

Wednesday

TO-DO

TO-DO

TO-DO

NOTES

164

Thursday

Friday

Saturday

TO-DO

TO-DO

Sunday

WEEK

Monday

Tuesday

Wednesday

TO-DO

TO-DO

TO-DO

NOTES

Thursday

Friday

Saturday

TO-DO

TO-DO

Sunday

WEEK

Monday

Tuesday

Wednesday

TO-DO

TO-DO

TO-DO

Thursday

Friday

Saturday

To-Do

To-Do

Sunday

Notes

My Wishlist

Record your birthday and
Christmas wishes here.

○ _____
○ _____
○ _____
○ _____
○ _____
○ _____
○ _____
○ _____
○ _____
○ _____
○ _____
○ _____
○ _____
○ _____
○ _____
○ _____
○ _____

WOW!

Gift Ideas

Do you have gift ideas for your best friend, parents or siblings? Write them down here so you don't forget them!

GIFT	FOR

Highlights

Write down the funniest and most beautiful moments of the year here so you will never forget them!

Mood Tracker

Track your daily mood for a whole month! Here are templates for two months. If you'd like to follow your mood every month, just copy the star garlands onto a new sheet of paper! A star represents a day. Set a colour for each mood and shade the stars in the right colour every day.

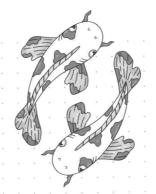

A DAVID AND CHARLES BOOK
© Edition Michael Fischer GmbH, 2020
www.emf-verlag.de

David and Charles is an imprint of David and Charles, Ltd
1 Emperor Way, Exeter Business Park, Exeter, EX1 3QS

This translation of MY MANGA JOURNAL first published in Germany by Edition Michael Fischer GmbH in 2020 is published by arrangement with Silke Bruenink Agency, Munich, Germany.

First published in the UK and USA in 2020

A catalogue record for this book is available from the British Library.
ISBN-13: 9781446308455 paperback

Printed by Polygraf in the Slovak Republic for:
David and Charles, Ltd
1 Emperor Way, Exeter Business Park, Exeter, EX1 3QS

10 9 8 7 6 5 4 3 2 1

Cover design and typesetting: Bernadett Linseisen
Layout: Meritt Hettwer, Bernadett Linseisen
Text: Mareike Schlesog, Greta Ruppaner, Marcelina Schulte
Product management: Marcelina Schulte

Image credits: Front cover: © Pixel Bits/Shutterstock, © nagisa/Shutterstock, © ATOMix/Shutterstock, © apricot/Shutterstock, © Sakarinn/Shutterstock, © 4clover/Shutterstock. Back cover: © 9'63 Creation/Shutterstock, © apricot/Shutterstock, © 4clover/Shutterstock, © Sakarinn/Shutterstock, © Jemastock/Shutterstock. Spine: © Rimmon1989/Shutterstock. Interior: © ATOMix/Shutterstock, © 9'63 Creation/Shutterstock, © Trung Anh/Shutterstock, © jet_stock/shutterstock, © cheheadache/shutterstock, © NextMarsMedia/Shutterstock, © Stavri Symeonidou/Shutterstock, © maxwindy/Shutterstock, © 4clover/shutterstock, © utako098/shutterstock, © Sakarinn/Shutterstock, © Andrey Apoev/Shutterstock, © Chuenmanuse/Shutterstock, © HH-Pax/Shutterstock, © Olexsandr Ozeruha/Shutterstock, © Lazu-tan/Shutterstock, © Issei Ariyoshi/Shutterstock, © HelloRF Zcool/Shutterstock, © rudall30/Shutterstock, © Mark Anthony Smith/Shutterstock, © Arun Boonkan/Shutterstock, © Linda Brotkorb/Shutterstock, © ommani/Shutterstock, © Jemastock/Shutterstock, © Lek Suwarin/Shutterstock, © yopinco/Shutterstock, © PT. Juzt/Shutterstock, © Vudgert/Shutterstock, © Salenta/Shutterstock, © chaffflare/Shutterstock, © marmileja/Shutterstock, © yopinco/Shutterstock, © Umaporn Thoonkhunthod/Shutterstock,© HappyPictures/Shutterstock

David and Charles publishes high-quality books on a wide range of subjects.
For more information visit www.davidandcharles.com.